THIS BOOK BELONGS TO

Merry Christmas

my favorite Boxer lover

Sara

Dedicated to all dogs everywhere who need and deserve forever homes.
- Ava and Prince

Ava and the Prince

Joy Sewing • Susan Barber

avaandtheprince.com

I didn't look like a fox.
Didn't feel like one either.

I wanted a home that would be a real keeper.

A fox ... really?

I had a place and a bed
and somewhere to lay my head.
But I belonged to a family who couldn't see
all of the things that were great inside me.

I liked to play. They didn't like to play.

I liked to jump. They didn't like to jump.

I liked to wiggle. They didn't like my jiggle.

I liked to lick.

They thought I was sick.

One day, they sent me far away
to find a new home where I could run and play.
I was scared. I didn't want to go,
but I wanted to be where I could live and grow.

At the shelter where I stayed,
were dogs like me hoping to play.

They wanted a home and a place to grow;
somewhere they could plan
for a better tomorrow.

I'm cute!

Pick me!

Hello!

A pretty lady with pretty shoes
saw me there and noticed I was blue.

Her smile was like sunshine over a hilltop.

She even smelled like lemons and gumdrops.

She liked my brown eyes that spoke without talk.

She liked my fur and the way I walked.

She looked at me. I looked at her.

She rubbed my head and played with my fur.

"You don't look like a fox," she said.

"You need a new name
that you will never dread."

"You look like an Ava, so glamorous and fun.
A dog that brings happiness to everyone."

Miss glamorous and fun

She took me home and gave me a bed
and a silver bowl from which I was fed.
She gave me treats.
She gave me toys.

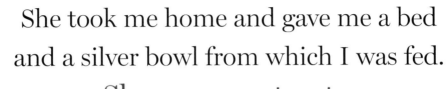

She said I could make lots of noise.

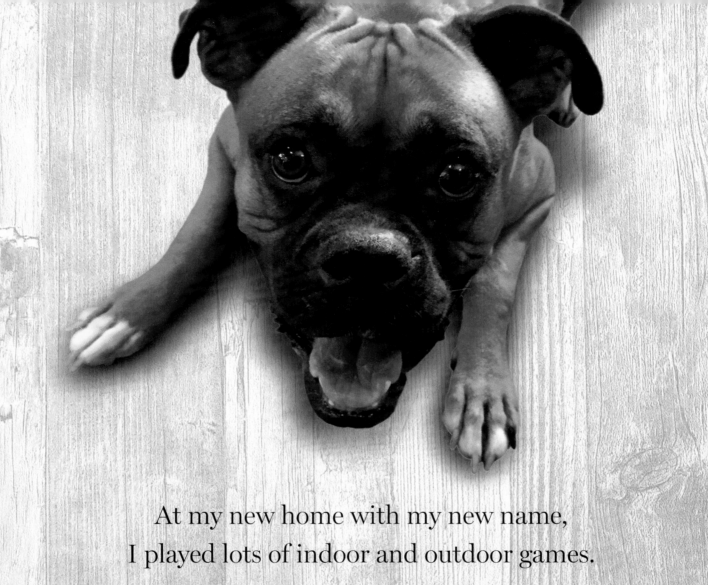

At my new home with my new name,
I played lots of indoor and outdoor games.

I wiggled and jiggled and licked and licked.

My new mom said I was a perfect fit.

One day my mom was busy on the phone,
so I decided to play on my own.

She liked shoes it was plain to see.
She had pretty ones
in pretty hues right in front of me.

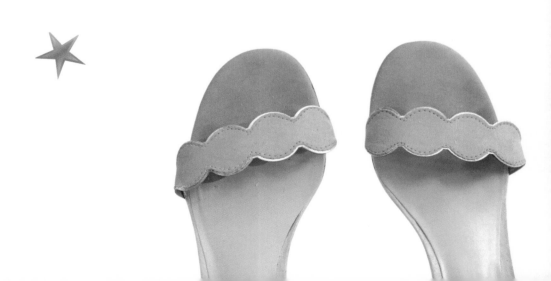

I liked her shoes too.

They smelled like melons, so sweet,

like one of those ooey, gooey, chewy dog treats.

I pulled them and twisted them to and fro.

I gnawed on the heels and chomped on the toes.

When mom discovered what I did,
she started to yell, and I ran and hid.

"You must learn the rules of the house right now.

You can't play with my things
unless I allow."

"You need a brother so you can run and play and make loud noises all of the day."

"A brother?" I asked. "But I like shoes and toys. I don't want a brother to steal my joy."

A brother?

Her mind was made up, she said with a smile.

She wanted another pup who had lots of style.

It didn't take long to find one who looked like me.
He had golden fur and brown eyes to see.

He had been wandering around without a home.
He was small, frail and so alone.

His name was Sam, like ham or jam.

He didn't look like a Sam.

But he was sweet like jam.

Mom thought about his name for hours and days.
Then she blurted,
"His name will be Prince, I say!"

*The one
and only!*

Prince and I spent time playing a lot.

We wiggled and jiggled and licked nonstop.

We went to the park. We played with our toys.

We dressed up in costumes
and made lots of noise.

At night, we cuddled in bed
and snuggled on pillows
that cradled our heads.

Mom said we were special — a family of three.
We created a home for us to be free.
Mom looked at me. I looked at her.

She rubbed my head and played with my fur.

She said, "A forever home is where
we all want to be, where love grows
and grows for eternity."

NOT THE END.

A Special Thanks

This book would not be possible without
the support of generous hearts who love books
and rescue pups as much as we do.

Our Angels
Yasmine Haddad, Brigitte Kalai, Sippi Khurana, Sneha Merchant and Neiman Marcus

Our Best Friends
Nancy Allen, Karina Barbieri, Mandy Kao, BJ Shell, Tammy Gee Su
and Lone Star Boxer Rescue

◆◆◆

Ava and the Prince: The Adventures of Two Rescue Pups
Copyright © 2019 by Joy Sewing. All rights reserved. ISBN 978-1-941515-92-1
Library of Congress Control Number: 2018952124

Published by LongTale Publishing
www.LongTalePublishing.com
6824 Long Drive, Houston, TX 77087

LongTale is a registered trademark of LongTale Publishing.

Story and Photography by Joy Sewing
Design by Susan Barber

First Edition
Printed in the United States of America